THE WITCH

By M C Menicou

Copyright © 2024 M C Menicou

All rights reserved.

No part of this publication may be reproduced, stored in a retrieval system, stored in a database and / or published in any form or by any means, electronic, mechanical, photocopying, recording or otherwise, without the prior written permission of the publisher.

The legend of Old Mother Ludlum has been told in certain parts of Surrey for as far back as the 17th century. It is said that the friendly old white witch used to live in a local cave close to the village of Frensham, where she developed an enviable reputation by lending local villagers anything they asked for, provided they return the item within two days.

The villagers would stand on a boulder on the entrance to her cave and clearly state what they required and once they had gone home, they would find the object waiting for them.

The legend goes that one day, a man visited the cave asking to borrow the witch's cauldron. Hesitantly, she granted his request, reminding him of the return policy; he must return it within two days.

For whatever reason, the man failed to return the cauldron on time, and Old Mother Ludlum, in a fit of rage, sought revenge on the man. When he heard that he was a wanted man, he sought refuge in Frensham Church, taking the cauldron with him, where it remains to this day.

Just like Julia and David in the story, you can visit it and see it for yourself. The cave is also still accessible.

Maybe you should visit it, too, but whatever you do, do not ask for anything. You just might get it.

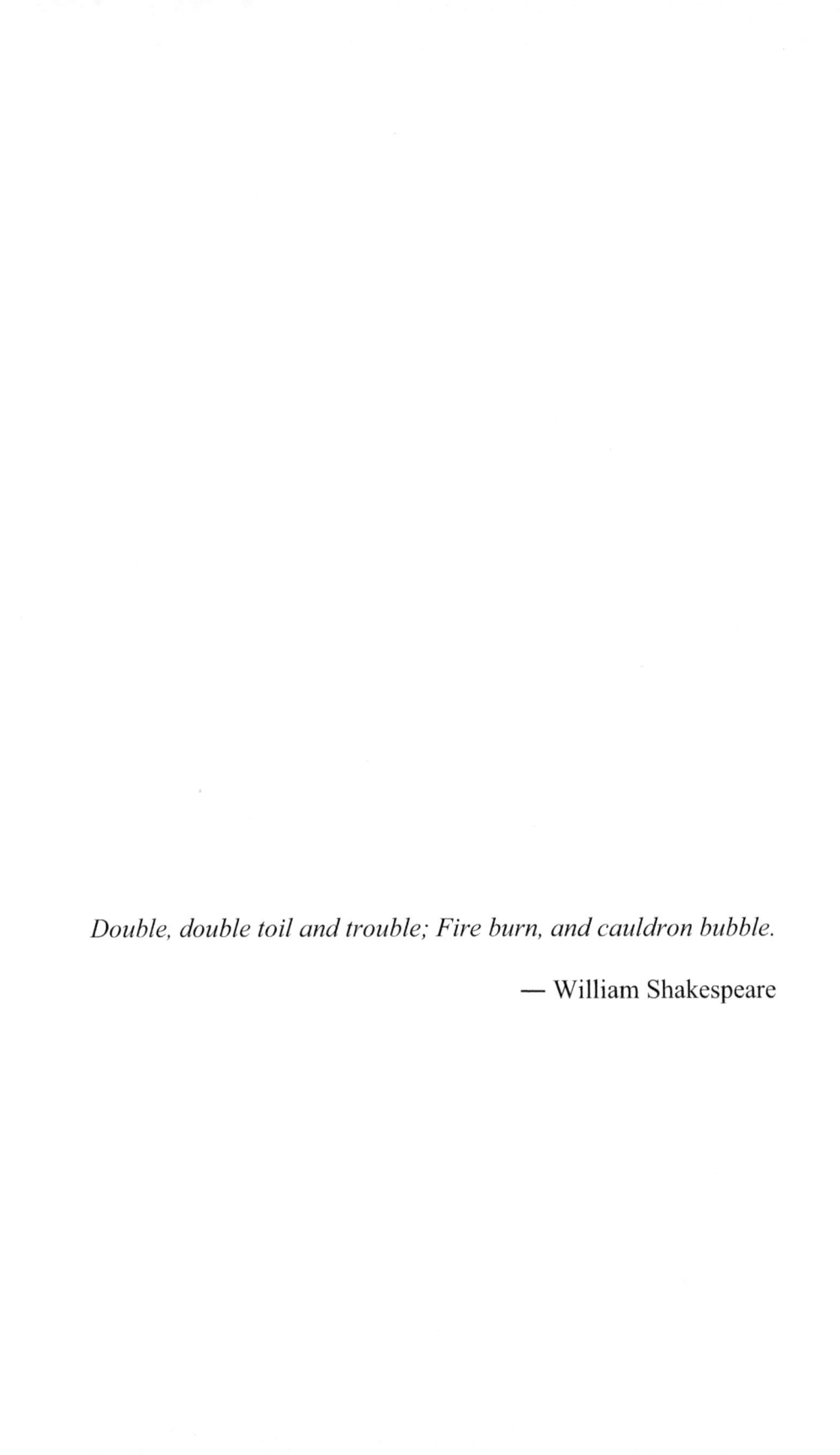

Double, double toil and trouble; Fire burn, and cauldron bubble.

— William Shakespeare

Farnham, Surrey: 1632

The wind howled relentlessly through the trees. It whipped dead leaves up into the air and made them dance in the firelight, their shadows moving to a silent dirge played by the spirits of the long departed. Branches crashed together on the limbs of the trees around the small cottage, an angry applause to some long-forgotten tragedy. Or maybe to an impending one, for there were three people standing at the door of the cottage, hunched against the wind and holding their cloaks tightly around them, their grim faces set as the shadows danced in the flames of their torches.

The one in the centre, the tallest of the three, took a deep breath before he raised his hand and gave a strong, loud knock. A few moments later, the door creaked open, and they were greeted by a rush of warm and inviting air before the face of Mother Ludlam peered out at them, her face creased from worry, her eyes red from tears. She stared out into the windswept night, knowing why her visitors were there, knowing the news they were bringing to her.

Silently, she drew the door wider and let them in.

Mother Ludlam remained silent as she lowered herself into her chair by the fireplace. A roaring blaze warmed the room and a pot simmered over the fire. Something bubbled inside it, and the room was heavy with the scent of herbs, as well as something else the travellers could not easily recognise.

"Well?" she barked. "What news?"

The man who had knocked on her door cleared his throat and stepped forward.

"We think we found the remains of a wolf attack near Waverley Abbey."

Mother Ludlam sat forward and gave him a hard stare.

"John Littlewood. You are an educated man, as some say. But there have not been any wolves in these parts for years, what makes you think that this is what caused the attack?" She spat the words out at him with a ferocity that made the man step back. His companions, younger than him, stepped back also, their faces draining of colour.

"Mother Ludlam, please, we are only reporting what we have been told."

Mother Ludlam sat back in her chair and nodded.

"It appears that the animal, be it a wolf or anything else, came across two people close to the river." He hesitated, licking his lips. He glanced at his companions, then sighed as he faced Mother Ludlam once again. "With all due respect, Mother Ludlam, all I can confirm is that two bodies were found." He paused once more and fumbled in his pocket. "We found this around the neck of one the victims." He handed the item over. Mother Ludlam took it with a stony face, her mouth set, her deep blue eyes shiny and wet. She held it, examining it closely, then she closed her fist around it and looked up at John Littlewood. Part of the gold chain hung out of her fist like a bejewelled rat tail.

"And young Rosa? What of my daughter?" Her voice was strong and stern.

"One of the unfortunate souls was a young a child." He hesitated again, trying to swallow but his mouth was dry. He eventually found his voice. "A girl."

Mother Ludlam closed her eyes. Tears spilled down her cheek and she stayed there for a long moment. At last, she took a deep breath through her nose.

"Leave me." she whispered.

The three men turned and walked out the door they came in, leaving Mother Ludlam to her thoughts. She sat there for a while, eyes closed, unmoving, and then began to whisper a chant. Outside, the wind began to howl even louder. The rain came, drowning the world.

Mother Ludlam suddenly opened her eyes and got up from her chair. Looking at the pot over the fireplace, she began to chant in a stronger voice.

"Spiritus noctis, veni ad me." She repeated this phrase as she picked up a wooden spoon and began to stir her pot, the bubbling mass turning over and moving quickly with every word she uttered. She stared into the concoction, and she began to smile as she saw the face of the one she called; he was coming to her. Mother Ludlam shrieked with joy, she cackled and laughed as she stirred the pot, steam rising up to the ceiling and, at last, she was standing before the Beast. It stood on two legs, strong and muscular. Its torso was that of a man with bulging biceps and a strong chest. Its head was that of a bull, with horns and snout, and the nostrils flared and steamed. A foul stench of sulphur and brimstone filled the room. But Mother Ludlam took no notice of either his appearance or the aroma of hell.

She bowed to it.

PART ONE: Frensham, Surrey: July 2022

It was just an old cooking pot, made of copper and remarkable in its un-remarkableness; it sat in an out of the way corner of the church atop a small stand on a black and white chequered floor. Unobtrusive, plain and old, yet it captured your attention in such a subtle way that you were unaware of the hold it had on you. It was made of hammered metal with two small holding rings on either side of the rim. It stood on three legs and measured around two to three feet in diameter. It was deceptively deep.

The guide showing the two people around smiled as he began talking about the history of this cooking pot, becoming animated. His passion for the story was contagious.

"There are many legends and stories associated with the area, folklore, if you will. This cauldron, for example, is alleged to have once belonged to a white witch who lived in a cave close by. The vicar may have more details, but this cauldron was used by the church for brewing beer, monks being the way they were," he gave a smirk at this remark. "But how it got here is an interesting story."

"What was it used for originally?" asked David.

The guide gave a wry smile and looked around dramatically, making sure there was no one within earshot. Satisfied, he leaned in slightly.

"Well," he lowered his voice, "local legend says that the white witch, known as Old Mother Ludlam, would use this cauldron for potions," the wryness of his smile deepened as he continued. "It is said that she would lend items, mostly utensils, to the local villagers, but they must return them within two days, otherwise there would be a price to pay." He paused here, watching the faces of his audience. Once his indulgence was fed, he leaned a little further and waited for them to lean in with him before he continued. "Those seeking to borrow an item would be required to stand on a boulder at the entrance to her cave, turn three times and state what it was they required from her. When they got home, the item would be there waiting." He straightened up, gleeful that his listeners had leaned in with him, and delighted when they adjusted their own postures at the same time as him. The guide continued in his normal voice. "There are many stories associated with how the cauldron ended up here. Some say it was a man who asked for the cauldron and did not return it within the two days, so he hid it in the church whilst Mother Ludlam gave chase. Another legend states that the Devil, in disguise, asked to borrow the cauldron, but Mother Ludlam recognised the Beast from his hoof-prints in the sand, so she refused. The Devil then stole the cauldron and the witch pursued him. Making great leaps, the Devil created a series of hills where his hoofs landed and where he touched the ground, the sandstone hills near Churt were formed. They are now known as the 'Devil's Jumps'.

"The Devil dropped the cauldron, and Mother Ludlam retrieved it. She put it in the church, out of the Devil's reach."

All three gave a nervous laugh at this.

"Anyway, there are many books on the subject if you wish to know more, and I'm sure the internet will prove to be insightful. If you follow me, the church's tower is very interesting, architecturally." He walked to a side door and opened it, Julia following close behind.

The cauldron held David transfixed for a moment, his eyes lingering over it, his imagination showing him the witch concocting a potion over a bubbling goo in the old pot.

Julia called him and he shook himself free of his thoughts, trotting to catch up with his wife and the tour guide.

* * *

Later that morning, sitting in a café together, a pot of tea on the table and plates of scones beside their cups, David was unusually quiet. Julia nibbled at her scone as she watched him curiously.

"What are you thinking about?" she asked, suspicion dripping in her voice.

"Oh, nothing. I was just wondering about good Old Mother Ludlam. I want to go and see the cave."

"What for? It'll probably just be an old cave with nothing much to see but a gaping hole!" She giggled at this, and David smiled at her.

"I really want to see it before we go. We've done everything else. Aren't you curious?"

Julia sipped from her teacup and smiled at him. Her cheeks produced the cutest dimples, and her eyes scrunched up, allowing a hint of her sparkle to shine through. For a moment, David was lost in her beauty, fascinated by her strawberry blonde hair cascading over her shoulders like a waterfall of sunbeams. And her smile, a trap for his senses, ensnared his heart. He was caught in her headlights, mesmerised by her magic, and he felt awe and wonder wash through him at this sight so bewitching, entrancing. He had no idea what lay ahead for them both, but he did not care; he knew what she stood for and what she did for him. In that moment, whilst she sipped her tea and nibbled her scone, his life was complete. And he could not resist the mischief that her smile promised.

"Okay," she said eventually. "But don't do anything stupid like you always do!"

"Like what?" he asked, feigning hurt in his voice.

"Like asking the witch for something! I know what you're like."

David laughed and took a big bite from his scone.

* * *

They parked at a country pub and went in to ask for directions to the cave. Compared to the bright sunshine outside, the pub was dark, compounded by the large dark wood counter running the width of the large room opposite the door. Levers loomed over the bar advertising bizarre sounding brews like 'Smokey Bishop' and 'Hog's Head', which did nothing to entice Julia in the slightest. The walls were coloured a dirty yellow, and she imagined that it was called 'Nicotine Sunshine'. There were tables and chairs lining the wall on either side of the door and booths were situated at the far end. The furniture looked old but sturdy, scratched with hieroglyphics that only a professor could decipher; or the local youths who put them there. The place felt old and it had a faint smell of . . . Julia could not name the distinct aroma. It was a mixture of stale tobacco and old alcohol. And grease. She could only imagine the kind of culinary delights one could order here.

Behind the bar was the usual array of stacked bottles and as they approached, she could see the small fridges on the floor with various exotic looking bottles inside. A chalkboard propped at the end of the bar announced a quiz night on Friday, proudly declaring in large, handwritten numbers, first prize twenty-five pounds and a free pint.

The landlord was a round man with a red nose and looked completely at home behind the bar. David walked up to the bar as Julia sat down at a table in a corner, watching him. Staring at her husband's back, a sudden chill ran down her spine and she shuddered involuntarily. A feeling of dread took hold of her and she closed her eyes, gently shaking her head. After a moment, the feeling disappeared, and she sat back in her chair. She didn't realise that she was gently rubbing her temple.

The feeling passed in an instant and she stared at David's back. He was much taller than her, stocky with a mess of yellow blonde hair. He had a confidence in him that she loved and he presented himself as such. He was a gentle giant and, most important for her, he made her feel safe and he made her laugh. Well, most of the time. His humour could sometimes be childish, but she did not mind that. She soon dismissed her feeling of dread as a manifestation of her own insecurities.

The landlord took his time getting to David, even though the bar was relatively quiet. He finished his conversation with a patron and was laughing loudly as he limped over to David.

"How are you today?" he said, throwing a tea towel over his shoulder. David couldn't help grinning at the cliché.

"A pint of bitter please and a gin and tonic."

As the landlord was preparing the order, David took the opportunity to ask for directions.

"Do you, by any chance, know how to get to Mother Ludlam's Cave? We've been trying to get it on Google Maps, but we can't seem to get any connection round here."

The landlord placed the drinks on the bar in front of David.

"Twelve pounds," he said. David fumbled in his pocket and paid for the drinks. As the landlord turned to the cash register, David asked again.

"Can you give us directions to the cave?"

The landlord turned and put the change on the bar next to the drinks. He left his hand over the coins and looked at David, his eyebrows knitting together.

"Why'd you want to go there?" He was almost accusatory, and David involuntarily leaned back slightly.

"Well, we're just passing through, and we heard about the legend, so thought we'd go and have a look."

The red-nosed man stared at him for a moment, then he squeezed his nose and leaned forward a little.

"I wouldn't advise it. Lot of strange things happen 'round there. It's haunted. Apparently. I don't believe a single word of it, it's just stories to scare the kids, but if you really want to go, you'd need to go down the road about a mile and a half." He pointed out the direction through the window. "It's sign posted from there. There's a small car park, and then it's uphill on foot. Don't ask for anything, though. Legends have a bit of truth in them, and this is no exception." And with that, he returned to his friend at the other end of the bar, leaving David bewildered.

Taking their drinks to the table, he sat down and stared at his wife, the shadow of a smile playing on his lips, his eyes twinkled. Julia gazed at him, her lips drawn into a smile. She rested her chin in the palm of her hand, her elbow on the tabletop.

"What are you thinking?" she asked.

He laughed. "You shouldn't ask questions like that." He picked up his pint and sipped it. "I was actually just thinking that as soon as work allows it, I'm taking you on a proper honeymoon. We'll go anywhere you want, anywhere in the world." His smile broadened. "The world deserves to see your beauty."

She could not help it; she found her smile broaden, and a little laugh escaped unexpectedly. That is what this man did for her; he could say the corniest, cheesiest thing in the whole world, and it would make her smile and laugh. This ridiculous man, this great lump of a man, that was as awkward and clumsy as a teenager, had the ability to make the world a better place to live in. His cheer would often be more cheese, she knew that, but his bad jokes still made her laugh. She loved him nonetheless; she knew they would be together until the very end.

She sipped her gin and tonic.

"It's okay, Sweetheart," she said. "I don't care where we go, as long as I go with you." Maybe his cheesiness was rubbing off on her; had she really just said that? "Now drink up, we're losing the day."

* * *

They found the path and followed it until they stumbled upon the cave. They couldn't miss it, really; the council had marked the entrance to the cave with two wooden posts along the path and a tourist information sign to the side.

Julia was impressed with it; an ornate metal gate had been erected at the entrance, patterned in the shape of leaves swirling around. As they got nearer, she noticed that she was wrong; the metal had been shaped in a swirling pattern, giving the illusion of waves crashing against the shore. Julia stared at it, marvelling at the simplicity of the design against the complex impression it gave. It seemed dissociated against the old cave, but it fit in with the surroundings. She supposed the gate was to stop vandals and graffiti artist from ruining the site, but even so, the gate seemed otherworldly, almost Celtic in design. She took her phone out of her rucksack and took a few photos.

David stood and stared at it for a while, a look of awe on his face.

"Amazing, isn't it?"

Julia turned her gaze to him and smiled. "It is, yes." She looked back at the cave again and took another photo.

David turned around and scoured the area.

"What are you looking for?" asked Julia

"The boulder where the villagers would stand to make their request," replied David. The boulder seemed to have been removed, but directly opposite the entrance to the cave, behind them, was a large tree stump. David smiled and jumped onto it.

"Oh, David, do get down and stop acting like an idiot!"

He only smiled at her and turned full circle three times. Julia sighed and rolled her eyes.

"Old Mother Ludlam, I need a spoon!" shouted David and then laughed as he jumped down. Julia glared at him and he laughed again. "It's just a joke, darling, no need to be so uptight."

She turned and looked again at the mouth of the cave, and she was overcome with dizziness.

"I want to leave now, David."

A cloud drifted across the sky, blotting the sun, taking away the pleasant warmth of the day. Julia hugged herself and she heard the leaves rustling as the breeze blew a little stronger.

"Just a moment, I want to see if I can look into the cave." He did not seem to have noticed the change in the air. He went right up to the gate and peered in. He got his own phone from his pocket and switched on the torch. The wind made his hair dance on his head.

Julia had goosepimples.

"What can you see?" asked Julia behind him.

"Nothing really, just an empty, shallow cave. I guess it could have provided shelter but there's not an awful lot of room in there."

"Come on, I'm not feeling too good."

He turned with a worried look on his face. "What's wrong, darling?"

"Nothing, I've just had a dizzy spell and I want to get back to the hotel before it gets dark."

"Okay, let's go," said David, putting an arm around her shoulders and allowing her to lean on him as they went back up the path.

They walked in silence until they reached their car and Julia, snuggling up against David, hugged her husband. The cloud had drifted on by the time they approached the small car park, Julia felt calmer and warmer. She closed her eyes and tilted he face towards the sun.

"I feel much better now, the walk helped clear my head."

David did not respond; indeed, he did not even return her hug. He stood with his arms limply at his sides and remained silent.

"David? What's the matter?"

She looked up at him. His eyes were glazed over, his face was slack, mouth slightly open. He did not even look like he was breathing. Julia, panicked, shook him, and shouted his name. He slowly lowered his eyes at her and his eyebrows drew together slightly, a look of vague recognition on his face.

"Um …" he stammered, and he turned his body back in the direction of the cave.

"David, are you okay?"

He stared blindly at the path they had just emerged from and slowly shook his head.

"Yeah, yes, I'm fine. Just had the weirdest feeling." His voice was low, almost a whisper, hoarse and gravelly.

With slow, deliberate movements, he reached into his jacket pocket and pulled out his keys. He had trouble pressing the fob to unlock the car and Julia stared at him, her mind a flurry of scenarios of doom and hospital visits.

"Here," she said, grabbing the keys out of his hand. "I'll drive," and she unlocked the car.

"Yeah, drive. I … I'll go, um …" he took a deep breath and shook his head. She watched as he slowly went round to the other side of the car and struggled to open the door. Eventually managing, he stared back in the direction of the cave once more and then slowly got into the passenger seat. Julia paused before she got in, glancing in the same direction, a shiver running through her body. Sitting in the car now, she leaned over and dealt with David's seatbelt. A brief struggle, it kept getting stuck as she pulled too hard, she finally got him strapped in.

She looked at him properly now. His face was drained of colour, his complexion almost grey. The worry in her increased. Panic set in and she did not know what to do.

She decided to drive back to the pub; maybe some refreshment would help him to recover. A cup of tea or coffee might help. The journey was silent, and the air was stifling in the afternoon sunshine. She rolled down her window and glanced at David. His face was pale, and his mouth hung open; she was reminded of the cave. He stared at the road ahead, but she sensed he was not really looking at anything.

By the time she parked the car near the pub, David was slumped in his seat, head hanging loosely on his neck with his chin hovering just above his chest. His eyes were closed and his skin appeared to have regained most of its colour. Julia thought he was asleep, and she stared at him for a few moments.

"I need a drink," he suddenly said.

Julia gasped in surprise and smiled.

"Welcome back to the land of the living," she said, relief softening her features as her smile broadened.

He yawned and looked up, turning his head left and right.

"You must have read my mind."

"Are you okay, sweetheart?"

"Yes, why do you ask?"

She looked confused.

"You really had me worried back there. You zoned out like a zombie. I nearly called an ambulance."

He scoffed and reached out to her, caressing her cheek.

"I'm fine, honestly. Come on, I need a drink."

They got out of the car and he reached out to her again, taking her hand and giving it a quick squeeze before threading his fingers through hers.

Inside, Julia insisted he choose a table and sit down whilst she went to the bar. Her gaze lingered on him as he shuffled onto the hard chair. He seemed so much better now, she allowed herself to relax a little. David picked up one of the cardboard coasters and tried to spin it on its edge. Relieved, she went to place their order.

The landlord was talking jovially to another customer, obviously a regular, and he was laughing as he came over to her. He glanced over at David, who was sitting at the same table they were sitting at before.

"How was the cave?" he asked Julia

"Oh, it was lovely; such a beautiful area."

"Yes, it's nice around there." He glanced once more at David and then stared intently at Julia. With a creased brow, he asked "Everything all right?"

"Yes. Why shouldn't it be?"

"Oh, nothing. It's just that your friend over there looks like he's seen a ghost." He scoffed at himself. "Anyway, what can I get you?"

"Do you have tea and coffee? Just one of each, please."

The landlord turned his back to her and busied himself with her order. Julia looked back at David; he seemed to be doing much better. The colour was returning to his cheeks, and he was flipping a paper coaster through his fingers. She glanced around the room. Not many people here; she guessed it was too early for people still at work.

Apart from the man the landlord was talking to as they came in, there was a young guy in a tracksuit and baseball cap standing at the other end of the bar. He was drinking a glass of beer and Julia was impressed as he finished the pint in seemingly just one gulp; until he let out a loud belch that disgusted her. Even more so when he laughed proudly.

Behind the young man, at a table by the window, an elderly gentleman wearing a hat and an old-fashioned suit sat nursing a pint of Guinness. His look of disgust at the young guy echoed her own and she smiled at him. He raised his glass to his lips and nodded back.

Tucked away in a corner, Julia noticed a woman; she looked ancient, her face full of wrinkles and her back hunched over. She was small and wizened. Across her table was a large stick, gnarled and knotted as though it was cut from a tree. As Julia watched her, the old woman raised her head and seemed to find her eyes, pinpointing her with the palest and sharpest pair of blue eyes she had ever seen. A fog descended over Julia's mind, and she lost awareness of her surroundings.

A clunk brought her back and she looked back at the landlord, who had put a pair of cups and saucers on the counter. The crockery, pure white against the dark mahogany of the counter, the dark liquid swirling round, gave her the impression of a pair of eyes searching for her. She almost did not hear the red-nosed bar tender.

"That'll be four pounds fifty," he said.

Julia, flustered, paid him and picked up the cups. As she made her way over to David, she glanced back at the corner table. The table was empty.

Confused, she put the drinks on the table and slowly sat down.

"What's up?" asked David.

Julia glanced back at the corner table again. The old woman was definitely not there.

"Nothing. I just thought I saw ...," she trailed off as she picked up her cup of tea.

David looked at his own cup and pulled a face.

"I wanted a beer," he said, looking like he was about to have a tantrum.

Julia laughed at him.

"I think a cup of coffee is better for you at the moment. You really had me worried back there. What happened?"

David sat back and closed his eyes. He ran a hand down his face and sighed.

"To be honest, I don't know. One minute we were walking back to the car, and the next thing I know we were here. Weirdest thing ever to happen to me."

They both sat in silence a moment, contemplating what he had said. In truth, Julia was extremely worried. She would have to keep an eye on him, make sure this wasn't the start of something serious.

"What were you looking at just now? You keep looking back at that corner."

"Oh, nothing. I thought I saw someone sitting there, but there isn't."

"Did you ask Mother Ludlam for anything?" the landlord called out from the bar, his round face laughing and his nose growing ever more red.

David laughed.

"Well. Yes, actually. I asked her for a spoon."

The landlord suddenly stopped laughing and leaned across the bar.

"Did you, now? Well, let's hope she didn't hear you."

"Why?" Julia tensed and felt her limbs loosen.

The landlord came round from the bar and sat down with them. He cleared his throat.

"What do you know about Old Mother Ludlam?" he asked.

David and Julia exchanged glances.

"Well, we went to the church where the cauldron is kept and the guide there told us about the legend." said Julia.

"Ah! Yes, the legend of Churt. But that's not the whole story, or even the true story." He leaned forward conspiratorially and looked at them both. "Old Mother Ludlam is a sad story, but one of evil too."

Julia shivered as she sipped her tea.

"There are two versions of the story they tell you at the church, I believe. One where someone hides the cauldron from Old Mother Ludlam, and one where the devil tries to trick her into giving it to him. Well, there is another version. The true version. You see, Old Mother Ludlam actually made a deal with the Devil. After a man took her cauldron and hid it, she became frantic, and so she called upon the Beast himself to find it for her."

"Was the cauldron that important to her?" asked David.

"Of course it was! She was a witch; she needed that cauldron."

"But she was a white witch," interjected Julia.

"White witch or not, she needed the cauldron and she wanted it back. By any means."

"How was it stolen in the first place?" asked David.

"So, this man goes to the cave, stands on the rock and asks Old Mother Ludlam for the cauldron. No one had ever asked for it before, and she was reluctant to lend it out, see. But she has her guarantee, her return policy. So, she lets him have it. Now, I'm sure the man in the church told you how this man didn't return it and hid it in the church? Well, when Old Mother Ludlam came asking for it two days later, he never told her where he put it, and she didn't even think to look in the church. So, she used her powers, and she summoned the Devil. The story goes that Old Mother Ludlam had some sort of control over the Devil, some kind of supernatural protection. Some would say that she promised him the souls of the young of the village, but nothing was ever proven. But that is a story for another time.

"Anyway, she made a pact with the Devil and ordered the Beast to find the man and her cauldron."

He paused at this point and stared at Julia and David. They were engrossed and were leaning forward, waiting for him to finish his story.

"And?" asked David, like a child waiting to see if the Handsome Prince would kiss the Beautiful Princess. "What happened to the man?"

The landlord sat back, his mouth a straight thin line, his eyes looking downwards.

"Well, you see, no one knows. No one ever saw the man who took the cauldron again. And Old Mother Ludlam died in her cave that very night." He paused here and looked down at his hands, playing with a nail on his finger. He rubbed his nose and sighed.

"There is one thing, though, that is peculiar. Every year, on the anniversary of the man's disappearance, a child mysteriously vanishes from the village. Every year."

The silence was now deafening. The air between them was heavy and pregnant and Julia felt her head begin to spin again.

"David, I think I want to go back to the hotel. I don't feel well."

"Would you like a cup of herbal tea?" asked the landlord, genuine concern in his voice.

"Thank you, no, I really want to go and lie down."

"Okay," said David. "Come on, are you okay to walk to the car?"

"Yes, I think so."

The landlord stood and moved out of the way for her.

"Are you sure there's nothing I can get you?"

"No, thank you, that's very kind of you."

David took her hand and put his arm around her shoulders, slowly leading her out to the car. At the door, Julia turned back to the corner table, and gasped. The old woman, with her stick, was there again, watching her.

* * *

"Honestly, sweetheart, I'm feeling much better now. Not sure what came over me, but it looks like it's passed now."

They were in their car outside the hotel. The day was darkening and the clear sky was a dark blue, holding an orange tint in the west.

"Are you sure? We should have stopped off at the chemist in the town centre."

She smiled at him and reached out, holding his cheek in her palm as she gently rubbed her thumb against his skin.

"I love you," she whispered.

He took hold of her hand and guided it to his lips. He kissed her fingers.

"I love you, too."

They got to their room, Julia laughing at something stupid David had said as they walked up the stairs. He paused at the door to their room before he unlocked it, staring at Julia.

"What's wrong with you!" she asked with humour glinting in her eyes.

"Nothing," he replied. He continued staring at her. "You are the most beautiful woman in the whole world, do you know that?"

She beamed and closed her eyes, wrapping her arms around him.

Once they were in the room, Julia threw down her rucksack and David went into the bathroom. She drew the curtains and went to pull the covers from the bed but stopped short.

"David?" she called.

"What?" he called back, his voice muffled by the toothbrush in his mouth.

"Is this a joke?"

"What?" She heard him open the door and come into the room, toothbrush in hand, foamy toothpaste dribbling from the side of his mouth.

"*That*," she said, pointing to the bed.

David stared. It took him a moment to see the significance, but when he realised what it was, his blood ran cold.

In the middle of the bed was an old, worn and weathered, wooden spoon.

Farnham, Surrey: 1642

"How long before the baby arrives?"

Old Mother Ludlam stared at the man as though a donkey had spoken. She stood up and walked over to the young woman seated on the old wooden chair and knelt before her, placing a hand on her stomach. She looked up and smiled, gently stroking her belly.

"Mary, you have a healthy baby boy in there. Now, I want you to come back to me," she turned and gave a stern look at the young man," alone, in three weeks. If you feel any pain or discomfort, come to me immediately."

"Thank you, Mother Ludlam," said Mary smiling.

The old woman stood, using her big wooden stick to help herself up, and turned to the young man.

"You stay away from her. I know you, Samuel Worsley, you have impure thoughts and if you so much as come near this woman once more, so help me, I shall call upon you with a might far worse than the Good Lord can muster."

Samuel was backing slowly away as Mother Ludlam paced towards him, and he fell over the low fence she had erected around her cave.

"Begone, godless man!" she called out to him as he ran down the path.

Mary was now standing beside Mother Ludlam and watched Samuel run as though the Devil himself was chasing him. A tear ran down her cheek, and Mother Ludlam took her by the arm and led Mary back to her chair.

"He won't be bothering you again, Mary."

"But what shall I do when the baby comes? He won't have a father."

"And better off he will be without that scoundrel ruining both of your lives. The rumours are true, my dear. He will not be faithful to you. He will cheat and fornicate with anyone, that one."

Mary's face crumpled and her tears came in torrents, her cheeks blushing, her eyes wet and red.

"Oh, Mother Ludlam! May the good Lord help me, but I love him so. What am I to do?" she pleaded.

Old Mother Ludlam stroked the girl's hand and hushed her. Mary suddenly straightened up.

"My father will be angry with me!" Panic made her voice tremble and her chest heaved.

"Young Samuel will learn the hard way, mark my words, he will regret everything he has done and he will try to worm his way back to you. Be prepared for that, Mary. And don't worry about what your father will say, I will speak to him and let him know what a cad that man truly is."

Mary, her tears abating, hugged the old woman and headed for the path.

"Hold on, Mary. Here's a few herbs for you that will help you and baby. Take a pinch from the white sack in hot water every morning before you eat anything. It contains wheatgrass and will help you get through the day. And a pinch from the green sack every night before you go to sleep. It contains jasmine and will calm you and the baby."

"Thank you, Mother Ludlam," replied Mary, full of gratitude, taking the bundle and going down the path after Samuel.

Mother Ludlam watched her go as she sucked on a piece of wood from the pine tree. She went back into her cave and tended her pot, simmering away over the fire, throwing in different herbs and leaves. Satisfied, she sat down in her favourite chair and waited for the concoction to be ready.

It was just before dusk that she heard the tread of someone making their way up the path to her cave. She waited patiently until the footsteps were right outside before she stood and watched Jacob Willow stand on the stone opposite the opening of her cave. He turned three times and cleared his throat before saying in a loud voice, "Please, Old Mother Ludlam, lend me three forks, three knives and three goblets."

Jacob stood waiting, watching Mother Ludlam, who nodded and turned back to her chair. She heard his retreating footsteps and then stood, leaning heavily on her stick, and went to the back of the cave, out of sight of the entrance and took out the requested items from a chest. She laid them on top of the chest, turned her back to the items and began to chant in a whisper. After a few minutes, she turned back to the chest and smiled.

The items were gone.

* * *

The following day, Mary and her mother came by the cave, full of excitement. Old Mother Ludlam heard their animated chatter approaching and she went and stood at the entrance to her cave, leaning on her stick.

"Old Mother Ludlam," called Mary's mother.

"Morning, Elizabeth, Mary. Everything good with you and the baby? Have you remembered to take the herbs I gave you?"

"Oh, yes, thank you, we came here to ask if you could help with something else."

"It's young Thomas Chudderley!" cried Elizabeth. "Joan's little 'un. He's disappeared!"

Old Mother Ludlam stared at them both. After a few moments, she opened the little gate and walked into the cave, taking a seat.

The two women followed and sat down with her.

"What happened?"

"Well," began Elizabeth, her words ready to tumble out of her mouth like a gushing waterfall. "Joan put the little 'un to bed as usual last night and they never heard a peep out of him, which was odd as he always wakes up in the night crying for his mum. He never liked being left alone, I always said, didn't I, Mary? I always said that that child would grow up tied to his mother's apron until the day he marries. Anyway, in the dead of night, there's a loud crashing noise, like a tree falling or something, and Joan goes running outside, but all is quiet, nothing is moving, and no one else in the village had awakened, so she goes back into the house and checks up on little Thomas, but he's not there!"

Old Mother Ludlam leaned forward, listening intently to every word.

"At first, they thought he had crawled out of bed, looking for his mum, but he wasn't in the house. Good Lord, they searched everywhere, twice, but the little 'un had just vanished!"

Old Mother Ludlam sat in her chair, sucking on the piece of wood. After a few moments, she picked up her stick lying at her feet and slowly stood up.

"Tea?" she asked.

"Oh, no, I couldn't possibly, I'm too afraid for that little boy. Look at me; my hands are shaking from the worry."

"Mother, please, you're getting agitated again."

Old Mother Ludlam had spooned something from her pot into a cup and gave it to Elizabeth.

"Here, drink this; it will help calm you down."

Elizabeth took the cup with trepidation and looked at the concoction. It was green and had an earthy smell to it. She looked up at Old Mother Ludlam who stared back at her. Slowly, Elizabeth took a sip, found that it did not taste as bad as it looked, and gulped the rest. She sat back and smiled.

"We were hoping you could help, Mother Ludlam, to locate the child," said Mary.

"What can I do about that?"

"Well, we thought, you know, with your special skills, you might be able to find him?"

Old Mother Ludlam stared at them again, her piercing blue eyes boring deep into Elizabeth's making her feel awkward and uncomfortable.

"I mean, if you can, it will help, you know, if you can find the poor lad."

"No."

Mary's eyes widened and her mouth dropped open.

"No, I cannot help. I can go and tend to Joan, she must be having some very strange feelings, but I cannot find the boy."

"Can't you even try?"

"Young Mary, have I ever been able to find anything in that way before? You know well my skills, and you will do well not to question me."

There was a finality in her tone that made her visitors know it was futile to argue.

When they had gone, Old Mother Ludlam went back to her chest and opened it. She rummaged around inside until she found what she was looking for. A piece of animal hide with something written on it. It was a list of names, and at the bottom, a name that was not there before.

Thomas Chudderley.

She sighed, put the hide back in the chest and allowed a tear to flow down her cheek as she went back to her pot.

PART TWO: Farnham, Surrey: 2022

"Look, it's probably a joke or a misunderstanding or something, try to calm down and get some sleep."

Julia was sitting in the chair opposite the bed. She was still wearing her outdoor clothes having only removed her overcoat. David was sitting on the edge of the bed, turning the spoon over in his hands. It felt deceptively heavy, but perfectly weighted. He balanced it on his finger and watched it for a while.

"You have to take it back," blurted Julia. Her voice was strained and her hands were visibly shaking. David looked up at her and gave her a cheeky smile and she couldn't help smiling back at him. "You're an idiot, you know that?"

"Yeah, but at least I did one intelligent thing in my life; I asked you to marry me."

"Yeah, you did, but then, I did one stupid thing in my life and said 'yes'".

The both laughed and she went and sat next to him, falling into his arms.

* * *

At breakfast the following morning, Julia was in a buoyant mood. David smiled at her as she chatted away aimlessly and when the young waitress came over to their table, she engaged in conversation.

Eventually, she turned the discussion to the topic that had been burning in her mind since the night before.

"Tell, me, Martha, has anyone been in our room yesterday? Only, we found something on the bed when we got back yesterday and wondered if anyone may have dropped it when they were cleaning the room or something?"

"I shouldn't think so, the cleaning staff are very good here and they take care in their job." She looked around conspiratorially and half-whispered, "The management take things like that very seriously."

Julia smiled at the young woman reassuringly and held her hand up. "No, I wasn't making any accusations or anything, it was just a strange object and we wondered if perhaps it was something that belonged to someone." She turned to David who just stared back at her with a silly grin on his face. "David, show her."

"Oh, yes, it's silly, really," he said, fumbling in his trouser pocket. He pulled out the old spoon and held it up like a prize.

The young woman shook her head. "I wouldn't know anyone that would have such a thing." She leaned in and took a closer look. "It's not one we use here."

David put it back in his pocket.

"Well, I'm sorry, but I don't think that belongs to anyone here, but I will ask and let you know."

"Thank you," said Julia. She leaned back in her chair, staring at the white tablecloth, thinking about what this meant. It was silly to assume someone would accidently drop a spoon in their room. A pen, maybe, or even a piece of jewellery; but a spoon? It was preposterous. Who carries a spoon around with them?

The thought spun in her mind, she felt tired and dejected. Could it really have been left by Old Mother Ludlam?

The question echoed in her mind until she felt a little pressure on her shoulder. Looking up, David gently squeezing her, she smiled.

"Come on, let's go and get our stuff," he said.

* * *

After breakfast and back in their room, David sat on the bed while Julia was busying herself in the bathroom, getting ready to explore the remaining areas before they were due to move on the following day.

David held the spoon, turning it over in his hands, looking to see if there were any distinguishing features. There were not any; it was just a plain wooden spoon, about seven or eight inches long and completely unremarkable. He heard Julia open the bathroom door and he quickly put it in his trouser pocket.

"What are you doing?" she asked, her eyes squinting and head held high.

David smiled and stood up.

"Nothing, darling. Where shall we go today? We could make our way to Guildford and visit the cathedral?"

Julia was putting on her coat and smiled at him.

"I think we should go back to that cave and return the spoon that you have hidden in your trousers." She gave a mischievous smile. "Or are you just happy to see me?"

They both laughed as David stood and put on his own coat.

"You are insatiable," he said, guiding her to the door by her arm.

* * *

"So, what's the plan for today?" asked David as he guided the car out of the hotel car park.

Julia thought a moment. "How about we go back to the church and see if we can find anything more about Old Mother Ludlam?"

"Really? I thought you'd have had enough of her already."

"I know you've got that spoon in your pocket, David, and I don't like it. It gives me a funny feeling."

David chuckled.

"Not like that! God, you are so predictable." She gave him a playful slap on his arm and he gave a comical yelp in response. She smiled. "I was just thinking that she is quite interesting, you know. I want to know if there's anything more we can learn about her."

"Okay, then, back to the church we go!"

They found the church empty. They sat at one of the pews near the back, in reverential silence together. David could feel the spoon in his pocket, heavy and awkward, pressing against his thigh. He shifted and tried to move it under the fabric of his trousers.

"What on earth are you doing?" asked Julia.

"Nothing, just trying to get comfortable. This thing feels like it's getting heavy."

"What do you mean? Oh, leave it, here comes the vicar."

He was a tall man, with wispy white hair atop his scalp, slim with gangly limbs. His mouth was just a slit under his bulbous nose and his dark eyes, which held a hint of wisdom in his otherwise old man appearance, fell on them both as he approached, smiling.

"Welcome," he said, extending a hand.

They both stood and shook hands with him.

"We were here yesterday and had the guided tour," said Julia. "And we fell in love with the place. It's such a lovely church."

The vicar smiled. "Yes, we have tried to keep it in its original state as much as we could. It can seem an impossible task, but I like to think we do a fairly good job." He looked around the building as he spoke, an air of pride in his voice.

"We were wondering, if it's not too much trouble, if we could see the cauldron again," said David. "We both found the story attached to it fascinating." He felt his cheeks grow warm and he looked helplessly at Julia, who only kept a fixed smile on her face as she waited for the vicar to answer.

"Ah, yes, the cauldron. An attraction set apart from the Good Shepherd Himself."

"Oh, no, it's not like that at all," Julia interjected, her tone almost panicked. "We're both Christians." She felt clumsy as soon as the words passed her lips. She felt herself blush and she looked down at the ground.

The vicar smiled and held his hands up.

"Please, no need to explain. To be honest, it is a very interesting little story." His eyes sparkled with an innocent playfulness and a corner of his thin lips turned upwards in a half smile. "I'm afraid I have a pressing engagement and must be going, but please, feel free to stay as long you want to. "

"Thank you."

As he was about to turn away, he stopped and turned back to stare at David with those dark eyes that seemed to know exactly what you were thinking. The silence between them was heavy and David felt he was about to be sent to the headmaster.

Julia glanced back and forth between her husband and the vicar. The silence was heavy on her, she could almost feel it crashing in on her. That sudden feeling of dread descended on her briefly and she reached out and took David's hand. He glanced down at her and smiled at her, giving her hand a little squeeze.

"Have you been to the cave?" asked the vicar suddenly.

David and Julia looked at each other frantically for a second before Julia said, "Yes".

The vicar continued staring at David.

"Is it getting heavier?"

David stared blankly at the man before him. His mouth fell open and he couldn't speak. Julia stared at her husband in confusion and waited for David to reply.

"Er, well, yes, actually," stammered David, putting his hand in his pocket and pulling out the spoon.

The vicar stared at it, eyes squinting as he examined it in David's hand. Julia noted that he did not reach out or touch it in any way. His eyebrows drew together as he locked his gaze at David.

"You must return it." He looked back at David, staring into his eyes, a deep look that seemed to be searching for David's soul. The sudden change in his demeanour shocked Julia, she felt her blood pumping in her ears. "Take. It. Back. Today. Now. You must before it's too late."

"What do you mean?" asked David.

"I must go, but if you value your soul, you must take it back to the witch before she comes for you."

And with that, he was out of the door.

David watched him leave in disbelief, the spoon in his hand.

"Crazy," he said.

Julia quietly sat down on the pew beside her and took long, deep breaths.

"Are you okay?"

She did not answer straight away but closed her eyes and tried to compose herself.

"Yes," she said eventually. "I'm fine, just another dizzy spell, that's all." She looked up at his face and smiled. "Can we take that thing back? Please?"

"We'll take it back later. Come on, we'll stop by the café when we're done here, you probably just need a cuppa."

He turned around and started walking down the central aisle.

"I just want to have a look at the cauldron again, maybe take a few sneaky pictures now that no one else is around."

They were alone in the vast church. Moments stretched between them, and Julia felt ... she was not sure what the right word for the way felt was.

Lonely

The word echoed in her mind, disjointing her thoughts. She watched as David walked to where the cauldron sat and thought about her life before she met him, how she was on a destructive path. She had been a capricious child and her teenage years only saw her rebel against her parents ever more. For a reason she could not fathom, she suddenly remembered a boy who went to the same school as her. What was his name? He was a bit scruffy, lived in a rundown area, and was the kind of boy her father would have loathed. She had tried to talk to him once, but he turned out to be a strange sort of person. She had asked him if he wanted help with some of his homework, they had had a science project due in and he was bottom of that class.

What was his name? John?

She remembered his reaction to her; arrogant, angry and offended.

What was his name?

She seemed to remember that a tragedy had struck him.

No, it was not John.

His parents died. Rumours were rife that his father had killed his mother and then hanged himself.

Jack! That was his name. Jack Harmon.

The name popped into her head so unexpectedly she gasped.

She watched David's back as he approached the small vestibule where the cauldron sat, and she wondered how lonely Jack would have felt after his parents died.

A shiver ran through her, and she shook her head, trying to clear her mind, and followed after her husband.

She found him standing over the cauldron, watching it with vacant eyes, the wooden spoon clutched in his hand. She noticed his knuckles were white and he had pulled his lips back in a half smile. He looked almost serene, contemplative. Lost in a world inside his own mind and she fretted a moment before she approached him.

"David," she whispered, tentatively reaching out to touch his arm.

He turned to her sharply and smiled.

"Oh, hello darling. Didn't hear you coming."

"Are you okay?"

"Yes, I'm fine. I was just, er, what was I thinking?" He stared at the cauldron a moment and chuckled to himself.

"David?"

"Yes, sorry, love, I was just wondering what this spoon was originally used for. Maybe good Old Mother Ludlam used it to stir potions in this cauldron; that would be something, wouldn't it?"

She reached out and took hold of the spoon. It felt warm to the touch, almost hot, and she tried to take it from him, but he pulled it back away from her and put it back in his pocket.

"Come on, let's go find a café. I'm worried about you; if you get another dizzy spell, we're going to the hospital."

"I'm fine, honestly. It's probably some vitamin deficiency or something. Nothing to worry about."

He looked at her a moment before he smiled and said, "We'll see. Okay, so let's go to the cathedral. Guildford is full of history."

He was halfway down the nave before she knew it and she had to rush after him.

"David, I think we need to take that spoon back. You heard what the vicar said."

He looked at her with vacant eyes, a smile playing on his lips, humourless. The silence spread uneasily between them, and Julia had the most peculiar feeling she had ever felt in her life. It struck her heart, and her mind echoed one solitary word -

...lonely...

She felt a sliver of ice run down her back and she shuddered.

"David, what's wrong?"

He seemed to come to his senses, and his old, playful smile was back on his face.

"With you here with me, absolutely nothing is wrong," he said and put his arm around her shoulders and guided her back outside to their car.

As she got in the car, Julia took a last look at the church before David drove off. She gasped. Standing at the door of the church, hunched over and leaning on a large wooden stick, was the old woman from the pub. She was watching her with a face devoid of emotion, her eyes burning into Julia. A feeling of despair overawed her.

"David, we are going to the cave now, aren't we?"

"In a bit, darling. We'll take it later on. Guildford is in the opposite direction, and the Cathedral closes at six." He reached and took her hand, giving it a quick, gentle squeeze before he started the engine.

Her misery abated a little at the promise of returning to the cave later that day. David guided the car onto the main road and the church was out of sight.

* * *

They walked into the cathedral and both were immediately impressed by the size of the interior. Great columns rose to the vaulted ceiling, as though the architect was reaching for God Himself. Both David and Julia involuntarily gave an audible gasp as they looked upwards, expecting to see the Throne of Grace nestled in the rafters.

A sculpture depicting bike riders stood just inside the entrance, as impressive as out of place in its surroundings. David stared at it in disbelief and Julia giggled at him.

"London 2012, the Olympics. The bicycle race came through Guildford."

David nodded, but still stared at the sculpture.

"Come on, let's have a look around."

They wandered into the great building, stopping to look at artwork on the walls, at objects housed in glass cabinets, the ornate round stained-glass window behind the altar.

As they gazed at the altar and the window, David reached out and took Julia's hand. She turned and looked at him; he was transfixed by the altar.

"Did you know The Omen was filmed here?" he said, without looking away.

"David! What is wrong with you!"

He laughed and turned to her, eyes locked on hers, and gave her his cheesiest smile.

"Just an interesting fact, darling."

They found themselves in The Lady Chapel. It was a small room, but just as grandiose as the rest of the building. And as they walked in, Julia felt awed by the room's austere majesty. They stood at the entrance in silence, then sat on a couple of chairs at the back of the room.

David leant forward and bowed his head, as though in prayer, and Julia smiled at his show of vulnerableness. As she looked up, she noticed they were not alone. A frail old woman sat at the front, her head down; Julia had the impression she was hunched more over due to age rather than prayer. Maybe she was praying for her back to straighten, thought Julia, and laughed at herself quietly.

She noticed that on the floor at the old woman's feet was a long wooden stick, gnarled and twisted. Julia shivered, something ominous had turned the air in the chapel cold and the old lady reached down and picked up her stick. Slowly, painfully, getting up from her seat, she hobbled to the back of the room. Her pale blue eyes fixed on Julia's, and she paused next to where she sat.

"Diabolus non expectant hominem," she said and hobbled out.

Julia was frozen in her seat. Her mind was numb. She forgot where she was, who David was, she forgot herself. For a moment, she just existed as a living thing, and Julia was just a figment of some animal's imagination.

Her mind began to spin, and she fell against David. He turned, and she was aware that he was saying something, holding her arms, caressing her face, and she snapped back. She felt groggy and nauseous, clung to David fiercely, unable to let go of him. She felt herself being guided up from her seat and slowly walking away. David's voice whispered in her ear the whole time until they were outside, and she was taking great gulps of cold air.

* * *

"How are you feeling now?" asked David. He had guided her to the Cathedral Café and managed to get her a cup of herbal tea.

"I'm fine, now, sweetheart, stop making a fuss." She sipped her tea. She could not look at him, her embarrassment was too great, but David reached and out took her hand.

"I'm taking you to a hospital. This has happened too many times for my liking."

"Stop fussing!" She did not mean to shout and she felt her cheeks grow hot as she looked around. No one seemed to have noticed, and she turned back to her husband. "I'm fine. Thank you."

He gave her a hurt look.

"You don't have to thank me, darling. I care about you. I love you."

She smiled at him.

"Sorry. I just need to sit here for a bit. I'll be perfectly okay in a few minutes."

He smiled back at her, nervously, and squeezed her hand.

"What shall we do after we leave here?" she asked. She was thinking of the old lady, but did not dare mention it. She was afraid that he would not believe her, think that she was losing her mind. Maybe she was. She decided that if she saw the old woman again, she would tell David.

"Oh, I don't know, maybe we should have a slice of cake to help make up our minds," he said, getting up. "What do you want?"

"Nothing."

"Really?"

"Erm, whatever you're having, I'll have a bite of it."

He came back with two slices of Victoria Sponge, and she laughed at him.

Beneath her laugh, hiding like the Loch Ness Monster, a little voice kept whispering a mantra, and she tried to ignore it. She watched David as he devoured his cake, and her cheeks produced the cute dimples he loved so much. But the voice persisted, trying to drive the smile from her lips.

"Diabolus non expectant hominem." It whispered. It echoed.

David was saying something to her. She watched his lips move, but could only hear a distant, muffled sound.

"Julia!" He was now kneeling beside her, holding her hand, his face creased with worry. She fixed her eyes on his.

"Julia, are you okay? Can you hear me?"

Her senses were slowly coming back as the voice began to recede. Just before it went silent, she heard a cackle; an evil sound.

"I want to go back to hotel, David."

He nodded and helped her from her seat, guiding her back outside and to the car.

Farnham, Surrey: 1650

Old Mother Ludlam was sitting by the fireplace in her cave, watching over her pot. She held an old wooden spoon to her chin in deep contemplation. She was thinking of the missing children in the village and of her secret involvement. Every year, when a child was taken, her guilt grew, but this was the price she had to pay for vengeance, for her husband and daughter. They were taken from her, nay, they were ripped from her beating heart. She knew that she could not see God in the same way from that day. An almost extinct animal had ravaged their bodies, eating them alive. God had abandoned her that day, and so she had abandoned Him. She had turned to the only alternative; she had had no choice.

The deal she had struck was that she would be left alone to practice her craft, without fear of the Witchfinder seeking her. And in return, a child would be sacrificed once a year. The pain she endured, still endures, will be felt throughout the village for eternity.

She was not prepared for the guilt, the hurt, of each passing year. A few years ago, it was her friend Mary's boy, whom she had named Robert after Old Mother Ludlam's husband. This had shaken Old Mother Ludlam, and the pain was as great as though she had lost her own daughter all over again. She cried with Mary, and with

Samuel, who had loved that child dearly. No sooner than the infant had been born and he had set eyes on him, had his heart softened and he had fallen in love with mother and baby instantly. They married that year, and they had been happy.

A child is innocent, the only sin was that of being born, and that was not the fault of the child.

There was nothing she could do, now. The pact was made, signed in blood, and she had no control over it.

Heavy footsteps from outside brought her attention back to the present. She listened but could not recognise the gait. She took her stick and painfully stood up, waiting to see who was approaching.

It was a man she did not recognise. He was tall, slim and he had a long straight nose. His cheeks were rosy, probably from the uphill walk to the cave, thought Old Mother Ludlam. He wore a blue tunic, dirty and coming apart at the left shoulder and a close cloth cap sat atop his head. She noticed he had long fingers, his nails short and black with dirt. She watched as he looked around the entrance before seeing the stone and climbing up onto it. He turned full circle three times and stood facing the entrance to the cave. She watched him as his eyes fell on her and he smiled.

"Old Mothe Ludlam," he called out. "Please lend me your cooking pot."

Old Mother Ludlam became instantly incandescent with rage. She took a step forward, her stick making a thump on the ground.

"Who are you? And why do you ask for my pot?"

The man jumped down from the stone and approached the wooden fencing. He took his hat off and bowed to her.

"Madam, my name is Jonathan, I have come to the village not so long ago, taking over as the cooper. I have heard that you will lend any object to those in the village in need, I need to borrow your pot as I do not have one yet, and I must feed my family this evening."

"No."

"But you must! I beg of you; my family need to eat, and we have nothing. I have already borrowed utensils and drinking vessels from almost everyone in the village. There are three young children at home waiting to be fed."

"You can borrow anything but the pot."

"I need nothing else; I implore you, your reputation is equal to none other than the Good Lord Himself; the villagers love you as they love their own families." He dropped down to his knees and raised his arms to her. "Here, I beg of you, to help my family, my children, please let me borrow your pot."

Old Mother Ludlam stared at the man, his beseeching was impressive, and his cause was noble. She thought of his children and was instantly reminded of the missing offspring of the villagers. Her heart jumped at the thought of his own family, starving, having to beg, and she took a deep breath through her nose. Noting how meek he must be to beg from the villagers, and to come to her in this fashion took the bravery of humbleness to achieve.

She relented.

"Go home, you will find the pot there on your return. Make sure you return it in two days. I'm sure my reputation has extended to the terms of my generosity."

She did not wait for him to respond; she turned instantly and began to empty her pot. She washed it out and hauled it over to the chest where she struggled, but eventually managed, to set it on the top.

She turned her back and began to softly chant and when she looked again, the pot had disappeared. She stared at the empty space for a long while before she hobbled back with her stick to her chair by the fireplace. She had an unnerving foreboding at what had just happened and, for the first time since her husband and daughter had died, she prayed to God.

She did not think He would be listening to her, but she prayed anyway.

* * *

The next day, Old Mother Ludlam went into the village. She stopped by at Mary's house who was busy preparing the meal for the evening when Samuel would return home from the mill. Old Mother Ludlam watched as Mary busied herself and chatted.

"You want to add some sage to that, it compliments the thyme and will bring out the flavour of those vegetables."

"I do not have any sage," said Mary with a smile.

Old Mother Ludlam reached into her cloak and pulled out a small bag. She produced a bundle of herbs and handed it to Mary.

"Here, take it, keep the rest and make your meals more palatable for your husband. Talking of which, how is everything?"

"Everything is fine, stop fussing. Besides, I have some news for you." Mary's smile warmed the old woman's heart as she stared into her eyes.

"Another boy," said Old Mother Ludlam, smiling and nodding.

"How did you guess?"

"I never guess; I can tell."

Mary chatted away happily, telling her guest of how life was becoming bearable and since she was expecting another child, Samuel and she were growing closer and more loving.

Old Mother Ludlam listened, and her soul soared at the news. When there was a break in the conversation, she asked her burning question.

"Tell me, Mary, what do you know about Jonathan, the new cooper in the village?"

Mary stopped and stood still, her face becoming nervous, and she took to biting her lower lip. Old Mother Ludlam watched impassively, but her mind was shouting warnings of disaster.

"Well, I don't know much about him, other than he came to the village about two or three days ago and instantly started to ask everyone if he could borrow things. But not just anything, he was seeking items made of gold and silver, as though any of us could afford such luxuries! But he managed to get mother's silver goblets which she had inherited, and some of Joan's silver forks. He promised he would give them back in a couple of days or so, but we still haven't got them. And, he has not been seen all day, the cooper's yard is standing empty. I fear he may have run off with our valuables."

Old Mother Ludlam stared at Mary, a fury rising inside her. Her heart sank, and she quickly stood up, leaning heavily on her stick.

"Are you all right? You have gone pale."

"I'm fine, I need to go. Thank you for the tea, Mary, dear, but I must be going now."

And without even a farewell, she was hobbling out of the house and down the road. Mary watched her go, fear for the old woman in her heart.

***

At the cooper's yard, Old Mother Ludlam stared at the empty workshop and the abandoned living quarters. She mumbled under her breath as she hobbled back towards her cave.

"If you can find him, bring him back here to face the magistrate," shouted Elizabeth from across the road. She was with Joan and both women had faces of thunder, the anger in their expressions surprising Old Mother Ludlam.

She ignored them and hobbled to her cave. She fed the fire and sat, sucking on her piece of wood to help calm her down. She had to wait until tomorrow night, when the two days would pass. There was nothing she could do until then.

* * *

The day and night passed quietly. Mary had come over to check on her later that evening, worried after she had left her house so abruptly earlier that day. Once she was satisfied that Old Mother Ludlam was in good health, and there was nothing she could do, she bade farewell and went back to the village, leaving Old Mother Ludlam to her thoughts.

The following day, the old woman stayed in her cave. She experimented with divining, trying to find where Jonathan had gone, but it was no use; her skills were healing and midwifery, not detection, and she gave up at nightfall, despondent and worried. She feared she had lost her pot, and without it, she could not help the village.

The evening brought with it the promise of the hour of reckoning. By the witching hour, if Jonathan had not returned, she would have no choice but to summon the Beast; something she had never had to do before.

The hours seemed to slowly drift by without any urgency, and Old Mother Ludlam was impatient. She sat in her chair for most of the evening, waiting, contemplating her life, remembering Robert, her husband, and Rosa, her daughter. When it had come to naming their child, Robert had wanted to call her Jemima after his mother, but Mother Ludlam had been adamant that the child was as beautiful as a rose and any other name would not befit her. After much arguing, for even in her youth, Mother Ludlam was a formidable woman, Robert relented, and Rosa was named.

A smile played on her lips at the memory.

Before she knew it, with shadows creeping around the cave, her fire was growing smaller, and she got up and fed it more twigs from the pile at the side.

The wind was picking up a little, and she felt that rain was due that night. She stood at the entrance of the cave and wrapped her cloak around her. There was definitely a dampness to the air, and she could feel the heaviness of the clouds above her.

The rain came a few hours later and Old Mother Ludlam sat huddled by her fire, wrapped in her woollen cloak and leaning towards the hearth. She muttered under her breath a curse on Jonathan the Cooper. A sheet of lightning lit the interior of the cave followed almost immediately by a thunderous roar echoing through the night sky. She grunted in approval; this was ominous enough for her to know that the time was right.

She sat back in her chair and closed her eyes, composing herself, before she took her stick and hauled herself painfully up from the chair. She took a deep breath.

"Spiritus noctis, veni ad me," she called out. Her voice was immediately followed by a loud clap of thunder that seemed to shake the cave. She held her nerve and stood, leaning on her stick. She called out again and another thunderous rumble shook the cave. A third time she beckoned to the Beast and this time, with an almighty thunderclap that threatened to tear open the ground, there he stood. Steaming snout, horned bull head and muscular torso. She noticed that one of its long ears sported a golden ring, which she had not noticed before. She found this curious and vain.

"You know why I have summoned you?"

The Beast nodded and gave a low, guttural growl.

"Then go. Find the man Jonathan and serve him the justice he deserves."

The Beast leapt past the old woman, ruffling her white hair as it ran out of the cave and down the hill in great leaps and bounds.

Old Mother Ludlam sat back in her chair. A tear crept slowly down her cheek.

"May God forgive me," she muttered as she closed her eyes.

PART THREE: Farnham, Surrey: 2022

Back in their room at the hotel, David sat on the edge of the bed. Julia was in the bathroom while he sat there, the old spoon in his hand, staring at it, turning it over and over. It looked innocuous, just an old spoon, made of old wood. Harmless.

Home

The word entered his head from nowhere. It sounded alien in his mind, spoken by someone else and it bounced in his head. Was it the spoon that spoke to him? Preposterous, he thought; nonetheless, the spoon seemed to weigh heavy in his hand. It was also warm to the touch, as though its temperature was slowly, steadily, rising.

He placed it on the bedside table just as Julia came back into the room.

"We need to leave early tomorrow," she said, pulling the bedsheet back. "It's a long drive to Yorkshire. And we need to stop off and take that bloody thing back to the cave!" She got into bed and began her nightly ritual; lotions and potions that would smooth her wrinkles; moisturiser for her skin during the night; and all the other things that puzzled him.

"David?"

He did not move. He sat on the edge of the bed, elbows on his knees, head bowed and breathing heavily. She watched as his back grew and shrank with every breath. She reached out and touched his shoulder. His skin felt cold, and he jumped at her touch.

"What's the matter?" she asked, concern etched on her face.

He was standing now, confusion on his face as he looked around as though confirming his surroundings.

"Nothing," he said, taking a long look at the door. He climbed into bed and sat up, still looking around. His eyes fell on the spoon beside him.

"David, you're scaring me. What's the matter?"

He leaned back down and rested his head on the pillow. As he moved away, Julia caught a glimpse of the spoon by the bed. Her blood ran cold, and goosebumps rose on her arms. She stared at it. It captured her mind, held it ransom.

"Nothing, darling, just been a long day. I'm tired, that's all."

He sounded tired. She watched him as he closed his eyes and lay still. Hoping that sleep would make him feel better. She took one last look at the spoon before she turned out the light and tried to settle down beside him. She tossed and turned for a while, but images of the spoon floated behind her eyelids, so she tried to snuggle next to David, but he was cold and unmoving. She turned her back to him and closed her eyes, trying to fall asleep.

She looked at the illuminated display on the clock beside her. 23:36. She should be asleep by now, they had to get up early. She tried to will herself to sleep, but when she looked at the clock again, it was 23:52. She sighed and turned onto her back. Beside her, David was breathing heavily, letting out a quiet snore when he exhaled. She reached over to him and quickly drew her hand back; his skin was freezing.

She sat up, staring at him in the dim light. He looked normal, sleeping peacefully. His lips moved silently, and he suddenly let out a little groan. She watched as his eyes started to dart left and right behind his eyelids.

Satisfied that he was breathing freely, she fell back against her pillow and closed her eyes again.

She must have dozed off, because a sudden banging at the door woke her up. Sitting up, wide awake and heart racing, she turned to David who was still sleeping beside her. His shoulder was cold to the touch still. It felt like ice and she recoiled as though her fingers touched fire.

Another crash sounded against their bedroom door, and she yelped. She watched in disbelief as the door handle began to rattle and the door creaked open. A red light burned into the room. The door continued to slowly creak until finally, it stood wide open. The red light danced behind the silhouette of two figures. One was small and hunched, leaning on what appeared to be a large tree branch. The other stood at almost two metres tall, broad-chested, arm and leg muscles bulging stark against the red light that seemed to flicker, full of life, fearsome, angry.

The small figure took a step into the room and Julia whimpered, her muscles failing her. She wanted to run, she wanted to run all the way home without looking back. She managed to turn and look at David, who had still not moved. He carried on sleeping, blissfully or ignorantly; she could not tell the difference.

"I'm sorry, my dear."

Julia faced the small figure that now stood by the end of the bed. The larger figure seemed to float behind the smaller one until they stood side by side.

"Payment is due for that which was taken."

"Wh-" Julia stammered. Her mind had failed her just as her muscles had.

The old woman, Julia could now see her in the dim red glow, raised a rheumatoid, bony finger and pointed at David.

"The time has passed and he has not returned my property. That means that he has stolen my spoon, and now he must pay."

"But, it's there," shrieked Julia, pointing to the spoon on David's side table. "Just take it back!"

The old woman pointed to the clock beside Julia.

00:02

"The time has passed for that, my dear. You will be unharmed; you have done nothing wrong. But your husband. He has stolen from me, and he must pay. I am sorry."

"Pay? Pay how? How much do you want? We have money."

The large figure grunted at this, and in the gloom, Julia thought it looked like the Minatour, except the head was not a bull; it was a grotesque caricature of the monster. The head was domed with tufts of fur patched across it; long ears protruded from each side, and they twitched nervously. Bizarrely, the left ear had a gold ring hanging from it like a pirate. Red and green patches littered the scaly skin; it had a snout with two large nostrils that seemed to be steaming, vapour escaping from them. Its mouth was a chasm, with thin, almost lipless edges pulled away to reveal three rows of small, sharp teeth, razor-like and deadly looking. Its wet and slicked forked tongue darted in and out, blood-red in colour. Staring at David with glowing red, manic eyes, hiding an intelligence. Julia sensed a hunger in that stare.

I'm dreaming, she kept telling herself. I'm going to wake up in a minute, probably screaming, and then David will hold me, and we will laugh about it, and I'll fall back to sleep in his arms.

Suddenly, the creature pulled the sheets off the bed and grabbed David's ankle. Fantastically, David still slept. Julia screamed, hoping to wake him, to allow him to take control like he always did and rescue her, like he always did. But the creature heaved David effortlessly over its shoulder and walked out of the room into the red shadows.

The old woman stayed a little longer, watching Julia scream.

Under her breath, she whispered, "I'm sorry", and turned, following the creature and David into the red void, the door gently swinging shut behind her.

Julia did not know how long she screamed, but by the time the hotel staff came charging into the room, her throat was raw, and she could hardly speak.

A call for help was last thing she heard before she passed out.

Later, she awoke briefly and saw a paramedic standing over her, calling her name and asking her to stay with him. Darkness.

Awakening again, she saw a white fluorescent light above. A nurse leaned over her, smiling.

"Where's David?" Julia managed to ask. Her throat still felt tender, and each word scratched itself out of her.

The nurse gave her a look of sorrow and touched her brow.

"Don't worry about that for now; you must rest."

"No, I must know. Where's David? Where is he?" Each word was agony, her throat like sandpaper.

Julia glanced around her, and her eyes froze on an object beside a jug of water on her bedside table. It was small and wooden. Normal, innocuous. Nothing sinister about it at first glance, but to Julia, it was an object of terror. It was an object that ignited a memory in her that shook her sanity and made her mind tremble.

She tried to scream again, but her throat seemed to have given up, and all she could muster was a raspy breath, escaping from her like a breeze ruffling dried autumnal leaves.

The nurse seemed to ignore her and adjusted something on the drip beside her bed.

"Shh, this will help calm you and baby."

Baby?

Julia fell into a deep, dark and dreamless sleep.

Farnham/Frensham, Surrey 1650

The rain beat down hard. Visibility was very poor, and Jonathan was having difficulty controlling the horse from his carriage. The laden cart jangled with the items he had 'borrowed' from the villagers, but he was worried that the large pot would fall out.

He had already passed Waverley Abbey and was now heading towards Tilford, the road was muddy from the rain and the horse was skidding and wavering on the slippery surface. He pulled over, stopping just before the bridge over the River Wey. He got down and checked on the horse, then looked in the back of the cart. The load was jumbled up but all present; he had not lost anything on the way. He pulled at the pot and made sure it was secure.

It was raining hard now, and there was the rumble of thunder in the distance. He went to the front of the carriage and looked back on the road. At that moment, there was a simultaneous clap of thunder, roaring far louder than the previous ones, with a strike of lightning. Then he saw something that froze his blood.

He was not sure if his imagination was playing tricks on him, but it looked like a giant man, with horns towering over its head, leaping over the landscape in the distance. Jonathan jumped up on the carriage and snapped the reins, urging his horse to run as fast as it could.

It was a slippery road, and the faster he urged the horse, the more he could feel the wheels slipping and sliding beneath him. He turned and looked behind him, but he could see nothing through the rain and night.

The feeling of fear, holding him in a vice, squeezing his heart and mind, urged him on, and the horse nearly flew across the path, heading for the village of Frensham. He knew the town and was familiar with the church there. The glimpse he had of the thing behind him put him in mind of the Devil, and so he headed towards the church of Saint Mary the Virgin, knowing that it would be empty at this time of night. The Devil will not be able to follow him inside, or at least, Jonathan hoped so.

As he reached Millbridge, there was another thunderous clap from the clouds, and he risked another glance behind him; lightning forked down from the sky, and he saw the creature, nearer this time, leaping in the air towards him.

He whipped at the reins ferociously, and the horse, sensing the fear of the man, ran harder, miraculously staying on its feet as it ran as fast as it could towards Frensham.

Frensham was just up the road now and Jonathan slowed the horse a little to take the turning. He could just make out the short church tower through the gloom and drove the horse even faster towards it. He pulled up next to the building and jumped down, going to the back of the carriage. Frantic, he quickly surveyed his haul. His eyes fell on the copper pot. His mind made the connection. "She is a witch," he muttered. The rumours he had picked up in the village were true. He hauled the pot out, thankful that he had stored it upside down. It would have been a lot heavier if it had filled with water.

As heavy as it was, adrenaline gave him the strength to carry the pot to the door, but it was locked. The door was solid wood and would not budge, the rain pelted down and Jonathan felt the cold from his wet clothes, which weighed heavy on his thin frame. Every drop that fell on him drew out what little warmth he felt. He was drained and panicked, knowing the creature was sent by the witch, that it was after her cauldron.

Looking at the building, he had an idea. Hefting the pot high above his head, he threw it at the stained-glass window. The window shattered, and the pot flew straight inside. Satisfied that he had put the pot out of reach of the Devil, he ran back to his carriage and tried to guide the creature away, whipping the reins and leading the horse onwards and southwards.

Three or four miles further along, the rain suddenly stopped. He slowed the horse down and looked around him. The night was quiet, serene, and above him, the moon shone. In the distance, he could still hear the thunder and the soft patter of rainfall on the ground, but around him, all was quiet. And dry.

A sudden roar filled the air. The sound was animalistic, but nothing like any animal he knew of, and the air suddenly chilled, his breath coming out in great plumes of steam. The roar again, closer this time, pushed him into action and he whipped the reins again, more urgently than ever before, and the horse, maybe sensing the change in the atmosphere, whinnied and ran on.

The rain stayed away but the chill in the air permeated and lingered around him. A shudder from the ground shook the carriage, and the horse rose on its hindlegs, screeching and whinnying in fear. The carriage was pushed forward by momentum and the horse skidded and fell on its side.

Jonathan jumped down and checked on his steed. It seemed unhurt, but he knew it could not go on any further this evening.

Another judder in the ground.

Another other-worldly roar, this time so close, he could feel the sound in his head. Jonathan was filled with a fear that took control of his mind and body.

Then, there was a sudden peace. The only sounds were the breathing of his horse and his own breath, fast and shallow. It seemed that the night had paused.

He turned full circle, trying to see where the beast was, but all was quiet. He managed to calm his breathing and almost convinced himself that he had imagined the whole thing.

He suddenly realised that he could not hear the horse's breath. With trepidation, he slowly walked around the carriage. What he saw rooted him to the spot. He lost mind, his awareness of the world around him evaporated; he felt his very soul shiver.

The Beast, the Devil, was standing over Jonathan's horse. It stood at eight feet tall, with muscular legs, the size of tree trunks and a naked torso rippling with muscle. But the head …

It was a bull's head, complete with horns. Its large ears, protruding from the sides of its head, twitched. A gold ring pierced one of those ears, and it glinted in the moonlight, mesmerising Jonathan. Its nostrils flared and steamed as it breathed, and there was nothing that Jonathan could do but stare at this grotesque monster.

One moment it was by the horse, breath steaming into the still air, and the next moment, it was holding onto Jonathan's throat and bounding upwards.

It jumped high into the sky and disappeared. The horse slowly and painfully got to its feet, its hooves clipping and clopping as the rain began to pour down once more. It carried on slowly along the path until it reached Churt. On the outskirts of the village, by the Great Pond, the beast appeared before the animal, scaring it. The horse, eyes wild and fear running through its heart, reared onto its hind legs and turned around, running blindly into the darkness, towards the water's edge.

* * *

In the cave, Old Mother Ludlam said a short prayer. She did not ask anything for herself, but for the souls of the children that had been taken over the years. She asked for reprieve from the grief for the families of the taken. She asked that Mary would have a healthy baby. She fleetingly thought of Jonathan, the liar and thief, but he filled her with anger. Did he deserve his fate? She wondered about that and decided that everyone decides their own fate. Even her.

She closed her eyes and waited. She did not know who she would meet when the time came, but that time was imminent, she could feel it. And she suspected she knew who would be waiting for her.

Her last thought was that wherever she would end up, it would be just deserved.

The End

Printed in Great Britain
by Amazon